Chaos at Christmas Cove

TINA-MARIE MILLER

Chaos at Christmas Cove

www.tinamariemiller.co.uk

Acknowledgement

Special thanks to Alexandra Miller, my wonderful, ever patient daughter whose editing and cover design skills have helped shape this festive novella.

You continue to be an inspiration to me beauty.
With unending love xoxo

For my dearest friends, Gill and Basil

et des fêtes de Noël chaleureuses à venir!
Fondest love xoxo

CHAPTER ONE

Maria took an unsteady breath - in then out - attempting to calm her jangled nerves, fearful that someone might walk in at any moment and discover her lurking in the shadows. That's if the pounding of her heart in her chest didn't give her away first of course. She leaned against the wall behind the door for support and formed her lips into an 'o' whilst continuing to breathe in and out as slowly as she could muster, *I'm really not cut out for a life of crime!* She checked her watch; *5.56 pm – two minutes to go.* She'd decided to make her move just before closing time.

When she'd ventured out that afternoon, it was with the aim of completing her post-Christmas errands. She had certainly not anticipated finding herself in *this* scenario and reflected on the events of the past half-hour. Frustration seared through her veins – a feeling that was quite alien for Maria - following her altercation with *him!* She was even more determined to complete her task now, come hell or high water.

It was seeing his assistant leave that had given her the idea to sneak back in, knowing that he was alone and therefore couldn't be in two places at once – or at least that's what she hoped.

She checked her watch again and fished her mobile phone out from her back pocket. With shaking fingers, she keyed in the shop's telephone number before pressing the mute key. Then, ever so slowly, she pulled open the door as quietly as she could and peeked outside, checking to ensure the coast was clear. As soon as she heard him answer the phone situated in the back office, she knew she was good to go.

As quick as a flash, she raced into the shop and headed straight towards the chiller cabinet where the box with the huge *M* scrawled across the top was nestled. With her heart still thumping wildly in her chest, she attempted to lift it carefully out of the cooler without being heard but was momentarily taken aback at the unexpected weight of it. With as much strength as her tiny frame could muster, she heaved it out and clasped it firmly in her arms before running towards the exit as fast as her legs would carry her. The automatic doors flew apart as she approached, giving her ample opportunity to make her escape and disappear around to the left-hand side of the building where her car was waiting. She gave silent thanks to the heavens above for having had the foresight to leave her vehicle unlocked, knowing she'd have a huge item to wrestle with on her return and quickly deposited her spoils before slamming the boot shut and jumping into the driver's seat. With closed eyes, she momentarily took a few more breaths as the shock of what she'd just done began to sink in. *It was rightly mine after all; it's not as if I've done anything wrong.*

The shrieking of her mobile phone ringing burst into her thoughts and with complete horror, she recognised the caller as *him!* With her hands still shaking from the adrenalin rush, she struggled to insert the key into the ignition before eventually managing to fire up the engine of her beloved Mini. Thrusting it into first gear, she drove out of the car park - even managing to cause the tyres to squeal dramatically – and raced out of the gates. It was only when she was well clear of Sandy Road and heading back in the direction of Holly Cottage did she allow herself to breathe a huge sigh of relief.

A smile stretched wide across her face. *Mission accomplished!*

CHAPTER TWO

'Hi mum, I was just about to call you actually as I'm closing up for the day now.'

'Oh Joe, I'm so glad I managed to catch you love. I've tried to call you a few times, but the line was busy. Don't tell me the last-minute Christmas rush has begun already,' Gloria Starr teased her only son.

Joe smiled. Despite his mother's ailments, she still couldn't switch off from the business for one moment.

'Not quite yet mum; it was just a wrong number that's all. But we have had a surge in footfall today. Which reminds me, there's a lot of shelves that need to be restocked but I'll get Katy on to that first thing in the morning before we open. It's been quite the day to be honest with you and I'll be glad to get home.'

'Oh dear, that doesn't sound very good Joe.' Gloria could tell by the tone in his voice that something had unsettled him, 'anything I should be concerned about?' She hoped it wasn't a disgruntled customer returning an inferior product. Whilst that didn't happen very often, she knew that all the remaining stock of it would need to be cleared from the shelves as a precaution, and that meant less sales.

'Not as such, just a misunderstanding really. Only I don't think I handled the situation very well at all. Not to worry though, I'll tell you all about it when I get home.'

'Well, I'm sorry to hear that. I'll open a bottle of something nice and we can chat about it over dinner. I was just calling to remind you not to forget my order. I'm sorry to nag but we'll need to get it sorted this evening if it's going to be ready for tomorrow night and I don't want to let Mrs Winter down at this late stage otherwise she'll be in dire straits, you know how it is love.' Joe did know, and he was looking forward to stepping in for Gloria the following night too.

'Don't worry mum,' Joe reassured her, 'it's all in hand. I've been carefully watching over it all day. Just give me a few minutes to close up then I'll head home and pick us up fish and chips on the way, how does that sound?' Even though he couldn't see her face, he knew his offer would be warmly welcomed.

'I don't know how I'd manage without you Joe; see you soon love and drive carefully.'

Joe began the short routine of closing down the shop for the night. There was an icy chill in the air as he slipped on his coat, and he was glad of the warmth from the fleece lining. He grabbed his keys before making his way back into the shop and over to the chiller cabinet to collect the box containing his mother's order as promised. Only when he peered inside, he was stunned to discover that the space in the cabinet which the box had occupied throughout the day was now empty. *What the ..?*

He stared in confusion and disbelief and absentmindedly scratched his head, bemused as the empty void in the chiller cabinet glared back at him. His gaze swept across the other cabinets in the chiller section before he began to search through them, moving onto the freezer section, just in case he'd misplaced the cardboard box with the huge *M* scrawled across the top of it earlier that morning, but there was nothing to be found. Irritation began to mix with bewilderment as he headed back into the office, wondering if Katy, the shop's assistant, had placed the order in there for safe keeping after his altercation with a disgruntled customer earlier that afternoon. The quick recollection of this event caused him to roll his eyes and shake his head before he resumed his search in the storeroom.

It was a good 20 minutes or so later before Joe realised that the box with the huge *M* scrawled across the top of it was missing. He was hot and bothered, having searched the shop, office and storeroom at least twice now until acceptance began finally to sink in. *Surely it couldn't have just vanished into thin air!* He remembered then that there was another area he hadn't checked - the bathroom facilities - which were only really used when the seasonal café was open. Despite knowing this would be the last place he – or any of the staff – would store a customer's order, let alone hide it, he searched it anyway but didn't find a thing.

Joe paced the shop floor. *Where on earth could it be?* He was certain the box was still there after that difficult customer had left earlier, *even though the cheeky madam had tried to take it with her!* A smile momentarily crossed his lips. Inwardly he liked that she was so highly spirited, *and very attractive too*. He mentally reprimanded himself for his foolish thoughts and quickly returned his focus back to the task in hand, although he was still struggling to make sense of how such a large box could seemingly disappear into the ether. Tiredness began creeping in and he rubbed his hands across his face in an attempt to invigorate his energy, but it was no good. He took the decision to lock up for the night, vowing to resume his search for the missing box in the morning.

It really had been a long and tiring day. It didn't look like it was going to get any better either given that he now had some explaining to do when he got home. How on earth was he was going to find the words to tell his mother that a 25lb turkey had gone missing? His only hope was that she wouldn't insist on calling in the police to investigate!

CHAPTER THREE

Maria heaved the turkey that she'd lovingly prepared into the oven, ensuring to close the door with the temperamental catch. She hummed along with the Christmas songs blaring out of radio as she placed the festive biscuits that had now cooled into an empty tin she'd lined with wax paper. The edible silver balls she'd gently placed onto the decorative white icing earlier, glistened from the glare of the fairy lights she'd draped around the kitchen dresser and sideboard. Pleased with her efforts, she washed and dried her hands before returning to the lounge. She shivered at the chilly air which encouraged her to add a few more logs to the wood burner before settling onto the sofa with the large glass of red wine she'd poured earlier. She put her feet up and snuggled her head into the back cushions, musing over the trials and tribulations of the past few hours.

Despite the stress of it all –it had taken ages for her hands to stop shaking when she'd got home –she knew that it had all been worth the effort to be on track with carrying out her late aunt's Christmas tradition, *even if things hadn't quite gone according to plan.* Recalling her altercation with the uptight manager of the local farm shop reignited her frustration and she took a sip of wine as her thoughts returned to the farce that had unfolded when she'd arrived to collect Aunt Ellen's order that afternoon.

Every year, as far back as Maria could remember, it was a Bright family tradition to prepare, cook and serve a full festive dinner at the local homeless shelter, the week before Christmas. It had been their way of giving back to a community that had welcomed and supported them through their own challenges over the years and Maria was determined to keep up this festive ritual. Not only was she honouring Aunt Ellen's tireless work for those in need, but she was also keeping Aunt Ellen's spirit alive. Only she hadn't expected that her first solo mission would take such a dramatic turn …

It was biting cold when Maria ventured out that afternoon, huddled beneath her favoured heavy, black overcoat, matched with a pink bobble hat, gloves and a woolly scarf that she'd wound snugly around her neck. The recent weather reports had predicted an unusually cold winter for Christmas Cove and growing fears of a major snowstorm bringing blizzard conditions with heavy snow and winds in the coming week were rife around the village. This had prompted Maria to make extra time to stock up on any supplies she might need during the holidays, together with collecting her Aunt Ellen's annual order for the homeless shelter's festive dinner.

Having to make several stops around her hometown had presented an opportune moment for Maria to catch up with several of her old friends. Whilst saddened by the death of her Aunt Ellen, they were pleased to learn that she'd moved back to Poacher's Pocket and settled into Holly Cottage, reclaiming her rightful place in the community. It was no wonder that by the time she'd reached the farm shop some while later, she was buzzing and bouncing on the balls of her feet as she approached the front counter, promptly catching the eye of the tall, dark and handsome stranger standing behind it.

'Hello there,' she greeted him artfully, 'I've come to collect my order. I telephoned earlier and spoke to your assistant who kindly promised to put it aside for me to pick up this afternoon. I got waylaid chattering I'm afraid,' she giggled, 'so I've come a bit later than expected. I do hope that's alright.' He couldn't resist picking up on her warmth and good cheer, prompting him to respond in a similar stance.

'Oh that was probably Katy, she's busy with another customer just now so perhaps you'll allow me to assist.' Maria suddenly felt shy and allowed herself a small smile.

'That'd be great, thank you. Actually, I remember now that there was another lady here the last time I came that dealt with the orders. Sorry I can't remember her name – it's been a while, has she left?' Now it was his turn to smile at Maria.

'That was my mother I expect – Gloria. She had a nasty fall a couple of weeks ago and is resting at home, so you'll have to settle for me instead I'm afraid,' he gestured towards himself as he spoke, grinning, 'I'm acting shop manager at the moment. Now if you tell me your name, I can get your order for you.' Maria was saddened to hear of Gloria's fate. A lovely, gentle lady, she recalled, who always went out of her way to welcome her and Aunt Ellen. She had hoped to see her again, especially now that she had taken up the reigns for organising her part in the homeless shelter's festive dinner.

'It's Maria – Maria Bright. As I explained on the telephone to your assistant, the order was placed in my aunt's name – Ellen Bright. She recently passed away, so I've come to collect it instead. It's all paid for of course. It's an annual order that she's had in place for years.'

'Ah, right, well we have a few of those – let me just go and check for you.' Joe already knew that there weren't any orders in that name because he knew that apart from the reserved items waiting for him to take home that evening, all the other orders were scheduled for either the Thursday or Friday before Christmas. Nevertheless, he went through the motions just to be sure and politely excused himself to recheck the order list and the stock room out the back in case Katy has stored her order out there.

Whilst he was gone, Maria took a moment to lap up the festive display of decorations that had been festooned around the store including a real Christmas tree – she noted – together with a full sized Santa figurine that cheerfully bellowed 'Ho! Ho! Ho! Merry Christmas,' at random moments. She absentmindedly wandered around checking out the delicious range of locally produced jams and chutneys and then strolled over to browse the baked goods on display, passing by the chiller cabinet along the way. It was then that she'd caught sight of the box with the huge letter M scrawled across the top of it and breathed a sigh of relief. *The assistant said she'd mark it up for me.* She returned to the counter almost at the same time as Joe reappeared.

'I'm sorry I can't see to find anything in that name,' he blurted, a tad uncomfortably. He hated letting a customer down.

'It's okay, I've found it!' Maria declared and nodded towards the chiller cabinets, 'your assistant said she'd put it aside for me.' Bemused, Joe came around the counter and followed her, intrigued.

'There you go,' she came to a halt beside one of the cabinets and pointed towards a box nestled there, *his* box. 'I'll just lift it out and then I'll be on my way.' As she leant forward to grasp it, Joe promptly stepped forward to stop her. He spread out both his arms in a protective manner in front of the cabinet.

'I don't think so,' he snapped. The smiley demeanour of just moments ago had quickly dissolved.

'Excuse me?' She felt a flush creep up her neck and into her cheeks as she challenged him, 'but that's my order – it has an *M* scrawled across the box for *Maria* – look. That's *me!*' she jabbed her index finger towards her chest to emphasise the point.

'But it's not an *M* for Maria though, it's an *M* for *Mum*,' he retorted indignantly, and Maria could see that he was getting flustered himself. 'This is my *mother's* order,' he continued, 'that I put together myself and I'm not giving it to you or anyone else for that matter!' Stunned into temporary silence, Maria took a step back and glared at him in utter disbelief.

'Look, I know you're only the *acting* shop manager, but I'm telling you that my aunt ordered and paid for those items in good faith plus I need that turkey for a charity dinner so if you don't mind, I'll be taking it home with me *now!*' She'd leapt towards him, ducking under his arms and grabbing onto the box.

'And I'm telling you this is not your order,' he repeated, turning around and holding tightly on to the box as if his life depended on it, 'it's been reserved for someone else!' By this time Katy, the shop's assistant, had finished with her customer and ventured over to find out what all the commotion was about. Maria caught sight of her, relieved that she'd soon clarify the confusion.

'You must remember speaking to me this morning,' Maria addressed her directly, 'I telephoned to explain about my aunt's recent passing and that I'd call in later on to collect her order.' Katy became uncomfortable and shook her head. 'Oh come on, surely you *must* remember. You told me you'd write my name on the box and put the order aside for me to collect later this afternoon.' But Katy remained adamant she didn't know what Maria was talking about. Joe cut in, desperate to resolve the situation.

'Look, I am sorry to learn about your aunt, really I am but you've clearly made a mistake here. Perhaps you're not thinking straight with everything you've had going on. I mean, I'm sure it can't have been easy for you losing your aunt so suddenly. Not to worry though, there's still time to place another order if you want to but you'll need to be quick. The last day for Christmas orders is tomorrow.' Maria was apoplectic. She glared at him for a few good moments more, quite unable to believe what was happening.

'But that's *my* order,' she jabbed her index finger towards him this time, but Joe maintained his stance as protector of the box leaving her no option but to accept defeat. *Even if I ordered another turkey it wouldn't arrive in time for tomorrow's dinner.* She couldn't resist throwing her best death stare towards him one last time before flouncing out of the shop and retreating to her car to lick her wounds and rethink her strategy.

Noticing the shop assistant Katy leave early gave her an idea. Maria knew the store didn't close until 6 pm because she checked the opening times beforehand to make sure she arrived in time to collect her order; *or so I thought!* She got out of her car and made her way back towards the entrance. A few other customers were milling about inside, and she could see the acting shop manager was occupied with another. She decided it was time to take matters into her own hands …

* * *

Inheriting Holly Cottage had come as a complete surprise to Maria, despite knowing that Aunt Ellen didn't have any other surviving relatives. Maria loved being back in the familiarity and comfort of her childhood home. A place she'd been warmly welcomed into almost twenty-five years earlier having arrived as a small, frightened and confused child. Aunt Ellen and Uncle Tony were relative strangers to her back then. But over the years, imbued with a wealth of love, support and encouragement, Maria had blossomed into an independent woman who went off to seek her fortune in the big city with their blessing.

Following Uncle Tony's untimely death just a few months after Maria moved away, she was tempted to return home again, fearful for her aunt's own wellbeing now she was living on her own. Aunt Ellen wouldn't hear a word of it. 'You've got your own life to carve out now Maria,' she'd reassured her, 'you can't be worrying about me. Come home to visit whenever you want but don't walk away from everything you've built up now; you'll only regret it if you do.' Although Maria had accepted her words at the time with a heavy heart, she now knew she'd been right to follow her advice. Not only had she created a successful business for herself – it was one that she could run from the comfort of her new home at Christmas Cove.

* * *

Maria took another drink from her wine glass. She wasn't proud that she'd had to resort to such drastic measures earlier and had been filled with intense remorse even since she'd returned home. Even when she was massaging butter all over the huge 25lb turkey and preparing all the trimmings for tomorrow evening's festive dinner, she was concerned that her aunt and uncle would have been disappointed at her actions. She felt certain that once the acting shop manager had spoken to his mother, she could explain the misunderstanding and all would be well. In the meantime, she was looking forward to her annual stint at the homeless shelter. It was going to be a night to remember.

Maria just hoped that would be for all the right reasons.

CHAPTER FOUR

On the drive home, Joe's thoughts travelled through a range of emotions but settled mostly on disbelief. He ran small scripts through his mind, trying to figure out how he was going to explain to his mum that her Christmas turkey had gone missing. Finally, he burst out laughing and shook his head, 'she's never going to believe this in a thousand years.'

As promised, he stopped off at the Christmas Cove fish and chip shop on the way home and was met with a cloud of warm air as he walked through the front door of Chestnut House. 'In here Joe,' his mother joyfully beckoned from the kitchen. He hoped her good cheer would remain when he imparted his news which he feared wouldn't get such a warm welcome. 'They're just saying on the radio that bad weather's coming in off the coast,' she poured out two large glasses of white wine and pushed one towards the dinner setting she'd laid out for him. 'Come and sit down,' she encouraged, 'I thought we'd be better off sitting in here closer to the Aga than in that draughty old dining room. Besides, I let the fire die down and I can't get it going again.' Joe bent down to kiss her on the cheek and then took out the plates she'd been warming from the oven and served up their supper.

'You're supposed to be resting mum, I told you I don't mind taking care of things when I get home. Let's eat and then I'll soon get it going again.'

'I only set the table love, don't fuss so. Sit down and enjoy your food, I've been looking forward to seeing you all day.' Joe smiled warmly at her; he loved her dearly and had been devastated when the hospital had contacted him a few weeks prior to say she'd had an accident. He didn't hesitate to travel back home to care for her and was thankful to finally use up some of the holiday allowance he hadn't touched all year. It was nice swapping the hustle and bustle of the big city for the familiar peace of the coast again. He hadn't appreciated just how much he'd missed it all. 'So as I was saying Joe, they reckon we're going to get heavy snow, might even be blizzards. Can you believe it? The last time we had weather like that was the Christmas you got that red bike. Do you remember love; oh how you loved that bike but you couldn't ride it for ages because of all that snow.' Joe did recall; in fact, he'd enjoyed a fabulous childhood and had many happy memories of good times spent with his mum and beloved dad, Malcolm.

Malcolm had been a real character. A cockney lad originally from the East End of London, he had somehow managed to find his way to Christmas Cove where he came upon Gloria. It was love at first sight, he'd told Joe, and they were together from that moment until his untimely death when Joe was 18. There was barely a day when Joe didn't think about his dad. Joe always looked back with fondness at the memories they had made together; the precious hours they had spent kicking a football around the garden or marvelling at crabs in the rock pools.

'We'll have to keep an eye on it,' Gloria continued, between mouthfuls of food, 'the weather I mean. We might have to close the shop – oh! I've just remembered, we've still got that pile of snow shovels, haven't we? Maybe you can fetch them tomorrow and start selling them again. Might make a good few quid on 'em too I reckon. What do you think?' Joe nodded in agreement while he tucked into his food. He'd decided that it was best to impart the news about his day on a full stomach, *an army marches on its stomach Joe.*

* * *

'Sorry love, can you repeat that again, only I thought I heard you say that you've not brought my order home because it's gone missing,' Gloria Starr looked up at her son in disbelief – but with a twinkle of mischief in her eye. In all the years she managed the family business, she couldn't ever recall a time when an order had gone missing. Joe raked his fingers through his short, dark hair nervous at what was to come. 'So what you're telling me Joe is that my turkey somehow climbed out of the chiller cabinet and did a runner?' With that, Gloria couldn't hold off a moment longer and fell about laughing. She was shrieking so loudly that tears of mirth began involuntarily running down her cheeks.

'I don't think it's anything to laugh about mum,' Joe retorted, slightly put out by her response. 'It's been a very difficult day actually. You seem to forget that I've gone from being a city trader managing massive amounts of foreign currency to dealing with stroppy, disgruntled shoppers!' Although somewhat calmer now, Gloria still had to suppress a few more chuckles.

'I'm sorry love, I don't mean to upset you. It's just that I can't believe what you're telling me,' she dabbed at her eyes and took a gulp of wine. 'That's better, now tell me all about this customer you had today and then we'll try and sort out the case of the missing turkey.' She listened carefully as Joe explained all about the young lady who had arrived shortly before closing time to collect her aunt's order. Joe relayed further how he had proudly protected the turkey with his honour causing Gloria to fall about laughing again as she mentally pictured her adorable son standing guard with a shield and sword in front of the chiller cabinets. 'It's a curious one, that's for sure,' she chuckled, 'what did you say her name was again – Bright? Maria Bright?'

'That's right, she thought the huge *M* I'd scrawled across the top of the box was to represent her name - Maria - but I tried to explain that in fact I'd written it to represent Mum as it was reserved for you.'

'Well she seemed pretty certain about it though, didn't she?' Gloria was serious now having had a moment to think it through, 'are you sure Katy didn't speak to her on the telephone this morning and is too scared to speak up and admit her mistake?' Joe shrugged his shoulders.

'You know her better that I do mum, it's difficult for me to say but this Maria was pretty adamant that she'd paid for that order – well her aunt had done so anyhow - and she put up quite a fight to claim it too.'

'Oh what a shame, poor girl! She might have got confused Joe, it wouldn't be the first time. Look don't worry about it but if she comes back tomorrow or telephones the shop again, let me deal with it, okay? I'm sure I can sort something out for her. I don't want any of my customers getting upset like that and certainly not feeling as if they've got to fight for their food! Whatever is the world coming to. Anyway, the thing we need to resolve now is where's my Turkey gone on walkabouts? I'm supposed to cook it tonight for you to take with you tomorrow. I don't know how on earth I'm going to explain all this to Mrs Winter. She was relying on us to bring another bird this year for their annual festive dinner.' This had slipped Joe's mind and he glanced anxiously at his mum who reached across the table and patted his hand comfortingly. 'Don't you worry about it love, worst case scenario I'll have to call in a favour from Gavin the butcher. He always orders extra like us. I'll give him a call in the morning and we'll sort it out then. If he can get one over to me, there'll still be time to cook it before tomorrow night.'

Joe went to bed feeling somewhat deflated. He knew his mum would have everything sorted by the morning, but he felt disappointed not to have been able to resolve matters himself. He'd mistakenly assumed running a farm shop was a piece of cake compared to his real job and it made him question how his mother coped with the burden of it all so calmly. He switched off the bedside lamp deciding those worries could be left for another day and snuggled under the duvet. His eyes felt heavy and his breathing slowed as images of Maria Bright swam before him until he fell into a deep sleep.

CHAPTER FIVE

Christmas Cove homeless shelter was bustling with activity by the time Maria arrived. Having wrapped up well against the bitter cold wind that threatened to blow in snow showers at any moment, she couldn't avoid the icy blast of air which stung her eyes, causing them to water and forcing her to dip her head as she walked back and forth, fetching and carrying the offerings she'd carefully packed into her car for the festive dinner.

Mrs Winter – who was dressed in Chef's whites matched with a pair of festive themed leggings and a garland of green tinsel wrapped around her ponytail - hugged Maria warmly once she'd deposited her coat, scarf, hat and gloves in the volunteer restroom. 'It's lovely to see you again Maria,' she greeted her with sincerity, 'and it's good of you to carry on your Aunt Ellen's work. She'll be sorely missed by so many but now she's passed the baton to you I've no doubt you'll do us all proud.' A wave of unexpected emotion swept over Maria and she had to take a moment which didn't go unnoticed by Mrs Winter who placed a comforting arm around her. 'Tonight is bound to evoke a lot of emotion for you, especially being the first Christmas without your aunt by your side but try to remember that you're not alone. We're all here for you; always.' Maria smiled through her tears and nodded in appreciation of Mrs Winter's kind words. 'Now let's get all this scrummy food inside shall we, else I'll be tempted to start eating it all myself!' Peals of laughter rang out as they carried Maria's contributions through to the kitchen. Mrs Winter quickly began unpacking the trays of roast potatoes and pigs in blankets that Maria had prepared earlier at Holly Cottage, whilst Maria lifted the turkey she'd cooked the night before out of the cardboard box she was reusing. She was just about to set it down onto the countertop when someone lunged at her from behind, almost knocking her off balance in the process!

'Hey! That's my missing turkey!' Maria spun around and to her absolute horror, came face-to-face with the uptight acting shop manager she'd clashed with the previous day at Starr's Farm Shop. He clasped his hands around the turkey – that was thankfully sitting on a plate and wrapped in thick, aluminium foil – and attempted to wrestle it out of Maria's hands. However, she was not prepared to give in quite so easily and held onto the cooked turkey for dear life. As they struggled back and forth, Maria strived to hold her position and out of sheer desperation lifted her right leg and stomped hard on her attacker's foot in retaliation.

'Get *off* me!' she yelled, grasping onto the turkey and holding it protectively against her. Meanwhile, Joe was hopping around, howling like a scorned child before he stopped to rub the developing sore spot on his foot.

'That hurt!' he yelled, 'and you should be ashamed of yourself; you're nothing but a turkey thief. I think you'll find that *this* belongs to me!' He lunged at the plate Maria was clutching onto with such force that she feared the cooked turkey would fly across the room at any moment, but she continued to maintain her stance and held onto the plate with all her might. She was about to open her mouth to offer up another pearl of wisdom in the form of a tart response when Mrs Winter appeared and beat her to it.

'Joseph Starr!' she screeched, 'what on earth do you think you're playing at. We're not at home to *Mr Rude*! You know we don't tolerate such behaviour from our guests and I'm certainly not going to make any exception for you!' Joe let go of the plate and dipped his head as a wave of shame swept over him.

'I'm sorry Mrs Winter, I don't know what came over me. I don't usually behave like that I assure you, it's just that Maria, er Miss Bright and I have met before, and I believe that she stole this turkey from me yesterday.' Now it was Mrs Winter's turn to look aghast.

'What? Stop being so ridiculous Joseph, who ever heard of such a thing. Two grown adults fighting over a cooked turkey, I've never seen the likes of it.'

'But it *is* mine Mrs Winter, look here,' he pointed to the large *M* that was still visible on the top of the opened, and somewhat now crumpled, box, 'I wrote that there myself. It's an *M* for Mother but *she* thinks I wrote it for Maria!' Mrs Winter shook her head and looked from one to the other.

'Tell me Joseph, was this turkey - that you believed to be yours - meant for tonight's dinner?' Joe nodded determinedly back at her.

'That's right.'

'And Maria, you've brought this lovely bird along for the festive dinner tonight too?' Maria nodded. 'So let me get this straight then, you were going to donate this turkey for tonight's dinner and Maria has brought it along for tonight's dinner is that right?' The two assailants exchanged glances before nodding eagerly. 'Then might I suggest that you put your troubles aside for the time being and just get on with the job in hand. It goes without saying that we're most grateful here at the shelter for your generosity, but you'll have to save you airs and graces for your own time. Now, quick sticks – we've got an abundance of hungry guests to feed and we're one turkey down!' She then gently propelled Joe towards the dessert section whilst Maria was left to continue preparing to serve the main course, together with the other volunteers who had also kindly donated copious amounts of food along with their time.

* * *

As the final serving of turkey dinner left the kitchen, Maria washed her hands and went to take her seat at the back of the hall along with all the other volunteers and shelter staff for the main event – the talent show! Not only did it give the guests an opportunity to digest their food, but also the local school could showcase their talents and present an evening of entertainment for their guests to enjoy before the final course was dished up.

This year's theme was the 70s – an era loved by many, including Maria – and as the show got underway the audience lapped up the nostalgic atmosphere.

Mrs Winter appeared with a tray of drinks and Maria gratefully accepted an elderflower spritz whilst enjoying Year 13's rendition of Dancing Queen by Abba. The whole room seemed to be singing and dancing along with them and the energy was electric.

Maria had already spotted where *he* was seated of course; on the end of the second row, to her left. She couldn't resist sneaking little glances in his direction every now and then. Only every time she did, she caught him glaring back at her!

* * *

Once the clearing up was complete, Mrs Winter sought Maria out to thank her for all her efforts and for her generous donations too. 'You've done a sterling job Maria, it's people like you who keep these facilities going. Can we count on your support again next year?' Maria nodded enthusiastically.

'Of course, I've thoroughly enjoyed myself. It's been such a fun evening and the entertainment was amazing.'

'Didn't they do well? They love coming here just as much as we love having them you know. Anyway, best you get off home now Maria. I don't want you and Joseph butting heads again,' she laughingly teased, 'although I must say that in all the years I've known him, it really is out of character to see him kick off like that. He's a good lad Maria and I don't know if you're aware that he's shouldering a lot of responsibility at the moment. His mother's none too well – which is why she's not turned up tonight - so Joseph stepped in for her. Of course, with Gloria being poorly that's also meant he's had to take on running the family business too, which can't have been easy given his high-flying job in the big city. That's enough to try the patience of a Saint, I'm sure you'll agree. Still, it's no excuse for bad behaviour is it. Anyway love, not to worry, it'll all be okay. You get yourself off and drive carefully. We'll see you next time.' They exchanged hugs before Maria could get a chance to respond. She gave Mrs Winter a final wave as she drove out of the car park.

Maria mulled over Mrs Winter's words as she drove back to Holly Cottage. She hadn't been *that* bothered by Joe's behaviour. In fact, it was nothing more than high jinks and she'd found it all rather amusing knowing full well that she'd played her part in exacerbating the situation. What had stuck were the comments about his mother, Gloria. She recalled that he'd mentioned something about it briefly yesterday at the shop, but now she feared his mother's health might be worse than he'd revealed. As she passed the moonlit bay where her Aunt Ellen had liked to swim in late summer, Maria felt a pang of the pain that was still so raw and wished she had been more understanding about Joe's situation.

Oh well, I guess I'll just have to wait until next year for our paths to cross again. But deep down, she really hoped that it would happen long before then.

CHAPTER SIX

To say the atmosphere was tense at Starr's Farm Shop the following day was an understatement. After a restless night's sleep, Joe decided to get in early and restock the shelves which miffed Katy, who enjoyed undertaking this task herself. The two seasonal part-time assistants, Bev and Linda, were due in that day and when they arrived did little to hide their disdain at discovering Joe was acting as shop manager.

Bev and Linda were long, established friends of Gloria and the three had met when their children had all joined the same school, almost thirty years ago. During this time, they had maintained a good relationship often socialising with their families in the evenings or weekends. In recent years they'd welcomed the opportunity to earn a bit of extra cash just before Christmas by helping Gloria out at the farm shop, which they put to good use mainly in spoiling their grandchildren. However, unlike Gloria, Joe didn't appreciate their seemingly endless tea breaks and chats and had to chivvy them along, which wasn't well received.

'We're expecting a large order in this afternoon,' Joe announced, 'including some extra boxes of festive cakes and biscuits so I'd like you to open up the café this lunchtime which will hopefully bring in a nice bit of extra income for us all.' A tight-lipped Bev and Linda exchanged glances of disapproval.

'Whose bright idea was that?' Bev challenged, 'have you seen the forecast – we're expecting heavy snow any day now. I'll be surprised if we even shift this lot.' She gestured around the now well-stocked shelves with her hands to emphasise her point.

'Try and maintain some seasonal cheer please Bev,' Joe sighed, 'I think our customers will appreciate a hot drink and a warm mince pie, and the weather should hold out for another day or two. Why don't you go and set the kitchen up? Once Linda's helped me unload the delivery, she can come and give you a hand.' Another round of glares were exchanged, whilst Katy kept her head down and began straightening out the counter preferring not to get involved. The sound of a rumbling engine from an articulated lorry pulling up outside the shop grasped their attention.

'Fabulous – looks like our order has arrived a bit earlier than expected. Get your coat on Linda, it's cold in the storeroom. Will you be okay to manage on your own for a bit Katy? It shouldn't be too busy at this time, just holler if you're struggling.' Katy nodded, inwardly relieved to have a moment to herself. Joe made his way to the office to grab his own coat and gloves when a thought struck him. He popped his head around the door to address Katy again, 'was that the phone I heard earlier by the way?' A hand flew to Katy's mouth as a look of horror swept across her reddening face.

'Oh!' she exclaimed, wide-eyed, 'sorry Joe, I completely forget with everything else going on. It was Mrs McGrath – she wanted to know if it was too late to place an order - I said you'd call her back.' Joe frowned and not just because Katy had forgotten to tell him about the call. Another more worrying thought struck him.

'Please don't tell me that you did take a call from that crazy woman we had in here yesterday and forgot to tell me about that too?' The look on Katy's face wasn't that convincing. 'Oh Katy, surely not!' Katy placed her head in her hands and began to cry – somewhat dramatically.

'I'm sorry Joe,' she wailed, 'I've had a lot on my mind recently, I don't know whether I'm coming or going at the moment so I can't say for certain whether I took that call yesterday or not to be honest.' Joe felt terrible seeing Katy like that. He hadn't known her for long but working in close proximity at the farm shop had created a mutual respect and he certainly took no pleasure from seeing her so upset.

'It's okay,' he patted her shoulder awkwardly not really knowing what to say or do. He wasn't used to dealing with upset such as this in his usual job and wasn't sure of the best action to take, 'if there's anything I can do to help,' he offered, more as a token gesture than anything else.

'It's our Benji,' she sobbed, 'he's been missing since last weekend and my dad says it's all my fault because I left the gate open.' Joe let this information sink in for a moment, uncertain where it was going.

'Oh dear,' he soothed, 'I am sorry to hear this Katy, I didn't realise you had a younger brother.' Katy stopped snivelling and glared up at him, her eyes red rimmed from crying.

'I don't have a younger brother,' she declared, 'Benji is our *dog*!' Joe blinked several times to cover his discomfort and give him a moment to think up an appropriate response.

'Oh, oh dear that is sad Katy, no wonder you're upset. You could always put up some posters around the shop you know, asking if anyone has seen your Benji. We're about to get really busy as you know and a lot of the locals will be in and out. What do you think?' Judging by the smile creeping onto Katy's face, she liked the idea a lot and blew her nose noisily in a paper handkerchief.

'Oh that'd be great Joe, what a brilliant idea, thanks. Is it okay if I use the computer real quick? I can log into my social media and get a picture of our Benji from there and put something together to print out. We've got plenty of ink in the printer, haven't we?' She promptly swept past him, took up a seat at the office desk and began eagerly clicking away with the mouse. Joe rolled his eyes, pleased to have diverted yet another drama and headed out towards the loading bay.

There was one thing that he couldn't shake off his mind though and that was his altercation with Maria. *What if she had been right all along and Katy had taken her telephone call yesterday morning?* These thoughts disturbed him. *Oh God, what have I done!*

CHAPTER SEVEN

It was the day before Christmas Eve and Maria was busy sitting at the desk in her small home office, creating a design for a new button range she'd been inspired to create following the 70s evening of entertainment at the homeless shelter's festive dinner a few evenings ago.

When Maria had first moved to the big city, having taken a job as a researcher for an online news agency, she decided to take classes in fashion and creative art at night school. Within five years she had created an online business for herself – Bright's Buttons – which had been steadily growing ever since, certainly enough to support her running it full time now. Having inherited Holly Cottage, together with a modest amount of savings Aunt Ellen had bequeathed her, she was now able to independently support herself.

A fluttering of snowflakes began clinging against the windowpane and caught her attention before the realisation set in that the first snowfall of winter had begun. She stood up to get a better look and gasped as tiny flakes fluttered from the sky before landing softly on the ground. The usually lush green lawn was already covered in a spattering of tiny white specks. At this, it wouldn't be long before the whole garden would be covered in a thick, white blanket. Maria shivered and went to place a few more logs into the wood burner, the action reminding her that her wood pile needed restocking. After wrapping up warmly in her coat, hat and gloves, she zipped up her warm winter boots and headed out towards the shed where she had an envious amount of logs stored.

She was quite puffed out by the time she'd shifted a couple of wheelbarrows' worth of wood for the fire, then stacked them neatly inside the front porch. In which time, she noticed that a good inch or so of snow had begun to settle. She stamped her feet a few times to shake off the snowy remnants and stepped inside the warm kitchen to remove her boots. She clicked on the radio and began heating up a bowl of left-over parsnip soup which she sat down at the bijoux kitchen table to enjoy, along with a few slices of wholemeal bread whilst listening to the local station's festive playlist. *It'll be lonely this Christmas, without you to hold…* the glam rock band, Mud sang out causing Maria to pause for thought. *It certainly will be a lonely and quiet Christmas for me this year.* She briefly lapsed into a melancholic mood before reminding herself that, despite being on her own, she still had much to be thankful for. She washed and put away her dishes, setting herself a goal to continue her work and aim to complete the new button design by the end of the day.

She was so focussed on the mission in hand that quite a time had passed before she noticed the flashing light on the answer machine. It wasn't until she sat back in her chair to stretch out her arms that the blinking on/off of the red light caught her eye; she certainly didn't recall having heard the telephone ring. *It must have rung whilst I was outside collecting the wood.* She reached over and the small, cosy room was soon filled with the warmth of a friendly voice – and one she didn't recognise at first - until she began to fully process the message and realisation set in. Fear gripped her heart and her hand flew to her mouth in utter despair. She reached over and with a slightly shaky hand rewound the message and played it again.

Hello Maria, it's Julie here from the farm shop – we spoke a couple of days ago? Only I noticed you still haven't collected your order, so I was just calling to give you a gentle reminder. What with this weather we're having, I don't want you to get cut-off and go without. I can ask my Terry to bring it over if you like, just give me a call back and let me know love.'

Maria didn't know what to think. She rewound the message and played it for a third time, but it didn't make the situation any easier. Admittedly, it had been a few years since she'd accompanied Aunt Ellen to collect the homeless shelter's festive dinner order, but she was *certain* they always used the farm shop in Sandy Road – *didn't we?*

She turned towards the computer and switched it on, quickly loading up a browser and typing *farm shop, Sandy Road, Christmas Cove* into the search bar at the top of the screen. Pressing enter promptly confirmed that there was not one but *two* farm shops in Sandy Road – The Old Farm Shop and Starr's Farm Shop. *Oh no! I must have got them mixed up!* She absentmindedly brought her hands up to her face in a prayer motion and was filled with dread recalling the shenanigans she'd created with the guy Joe who was acting as shop manager at Starr's Farm Shop. *I insisted that he'd made a mistake!* She groaned as images of the fracas that had followed in the kitchen at the homeless shelter swept into her mind. *Oh good lord, what have I done!* She covered her face with her hands and felt like crying but as quick as that thought appeared she quashed it; *that's not going to solve anything.*

There was only one course of action left open to her and Maria knew she'd have to take it no matter what. *I just hope he's more receptive than the last time we met!*

CHAPTER EIGHT

'Joe the coffee machine's playing up,' Bev complained – and not for the first time that afternoon either. The lunchtime rush was well underway, and they all had their hands full serving customers. Quite a queue had formed, and the café was nearly up to occupancy.

'I'll be with you in a minute Bev,' Joe replied as patiently as he could between clenched teeth.

'I'm not surprised to be honest,' she rambled on unhelpfully, 'you need to give these industrial machines time to warm up before using them. It's been sitting out of action for months.' Knowing this wasn't something that would make the shop's customers cheery, Joe managed to wrestle a CD into the sound system and melodic festive tunes soon filled the air whilst he dashed over to assist Bev with her coffee machine drama.

'Oh Joe,' gasped Linda, 'I'm glad you're here – don't suppose you know where the spare napkins are? We've run out and I haven't had a minute to fetch some more.'

'Be with you in a second Linda,' he smiled through gritted teeth, whilst his stress levels rose up another notch.

'I don't think you're doing it right,' Bev interjected and tried to take over. It took all of Joe's strength not to swat her hand away.

'Just give me a moment Bev,' he pleaded whilst he performed a quick examination. 'it looks like the filter is all clogged up. Can you give it a thorough clean out and try again? I'll make time to descale it before I leave tonight. Otherwise you'll have to use the kettle from the staff room. Is that okay?' He was relieved that Bev seemed happy to accept his assessment, then rushed off to the stock room to look for more napkins. Once he'd delivered these to Linda, he returned to the shop's counter where Katy was doing a sterling job managing to keep the queue flowing without any customer frustrations breaking out, *we certainly don't want a repeat of yesterday's antics.*

It was almost 6.30 pm by the time Joe closed up for the night, having thanked his staff for all their hard work in supporting his idea to add the burden of opening the café together with the overflow of customers the festive season always drew in. Bev and Linda had actually praised his decision *and* gave him a friendly hug before they left. Their kindness had boosted his spirits and helped to relieve some of the stress he'd been battling throughout the day, fearful that he was going to mess things up. He'd been so keen to return to Christmas Cove and help out his mother whilst she recuperated from her fall. In fact, he'd welcomed it as he'd long needed a break from his busy city job as a foreign exchange trader. He quite like the idea of running a small farm shop by the sea for a few weeks but the reality had been far from what he'd expected. He wasn't sure he was cut out for it.

He made his way towards the café with a heavy heart to take care of descaling the coffee machine. Everything needed to be in working order for the shop's busiest day of the year – Christmas Eve. His heart fluttered with excitement at what the day might bring too. It had already begun to snow, and he wondered if it would be deep enough to build a snowman which caused him to laugh. 'You're a big kid Joseph Starr,' he said out loud, indulging his inner child as he recalled many happy memories from playing in the snow with his friends. It was almost 8 pm by the time he had the farm shop fully organised for the following day. As he stepped outside, he was surprised to discover that the snow fall was already an inch or so deep and flakes were still furiously descending from the sky. *If it carries on like this, I'll be surprised if I make it off the driveway tomorrow morning, let alone be here to welcome any customers!* He cleared away the ice and snow obstructing the windows of his car before settling into the driver's seat and heading towards home.

Having decided to park his car in the garage overnight to save time clearing the snow away again in the morning, he didn't notice the strange car parked in the far corner. It was a bit of a faff getting the garage door open, but he managed it and left the car securely locked up for the night before venturing inside. He welcomed the burst of warm air as he stepped inside Chestnut House and took a few minutes to untie his shoes and shake away the snow from his coat and scarf. It was at this point that he realised he could hear voices and went to join his mother in the front room, keen to discover who their guest could be.

Only when he walked in and his eyes fell upon a by-now familiar figure, he opened his mouth and lashed out before he'd had a chance to put his brain in gear. 'Oh good God,' he groaned, 'what the hell are you doing here!'

CHAPTER NINE

It had taken Maria a while to get her act together. She took no joy from the realisation that she made a huge mistake and that as a consequence, she'd caused unnecessary distress to many people.

It would be easy to use the sudden death of Aunt Ellen as an excuse to explain her misguided actions, but this simply wasn't true, and Maria wasn't one to play at being the victim either.

The reality was that she hadn't been back to visit Aunt Ellen since last Christmas and the year before that she'd only managed to come home for a brief week in July. She'd been so wrapped up in developing her business that she'd been blindsided to the things that were most important to her. Enjoying long conversations with her aunt regularly by telephone wasn't the same. Whilst Maria always arrived home in time to help volunteer at the homeless shelter's festive dinner with her aunt – and stayed for a week or so afterwards - it was Aunt Ellen who put in all the effort shopping for their contribution and preparing the festive food in advance. All Maria really did was turn up, drive them to the shelter and then help serve everything up.

Now she was left to tackle the responsibility on her own, she'd made some assumptions which had clearly turned out to be completely incorrect and it was time to put things right. She buttoned up her thick, wool coat and slipped on a pair of fur lined boots, not forgetting her woolly hat and scarf, and headed out to her car to drive to Sandy Road and this time to the *correct* farm shop.

* * *

As she retraced her journey from the day before, she took some solace in noticing that Starr's Farm Shop was the first store she passed along Sandy Road. It was, she reasoned, an easy assumption for anyone to make if you're not that familiar with the local area — *and don't know that there is not one but two farm shops situated along the same road!* She continued along, not appreciating that Sandy Road stretched quite a distance before she finally came upon the Old Farm Shop. A craggy, wooden signpost that had seen better days suddenly came into view. Its faded, tired white lettering pointed towards a muddy track, where the shop was tucked away. She tentatively followed its direction, until the whitewashed walls of a somewhat dishevelled looking building loomed ahead — a far cry from her recollection of previous visits she'd taken here with Aunt Ellen. A few inches of snow had settled overnight and her boots crunched along the pathway as she made her way inside instantly recognising the owner, Julie. Despite the rather bedraggled façade, the inside of the shop was much brighter and well organised. Julie looked up and a warm smile spread across her face as she stepped around the shop's counter and came forward with open arms to welcome Maria inside.

Maria chose not to go into too much detail as to why she was delayed in collecting her order and thankfully Julie didn't ask much about it either. It was bad enough that she still had a wrong to put right without reliving the chaotic events that had ensued due to her ineptitude to have properly checked the original paperwork beforehand. Instead, she took a moment to appreciate Julie's kind words as she expressed her genuine condolence for Maria's loss. 'Your Aunt Ellen had been a loyal customer of ours for as many years as I can remember,' she reflected, 'and I shall always remember her with fondness.' Sensing Julie's affable mood, Maria decided it would do no harm to try and further her own cause.

'I don't suppose you happen to know the lady who owns the farm shop further along Sandy Road, do you?' Maria enquired innocently, having already devised a possible way to make amends.

'Gloria you mean? Of course I do – we've been friends for years. I was sorry to hear that she'd had a nasty fall recently, poor love, although her son's been helping out whilst she's out of action I understand. What a good lad he is too. I can't see either of mine stepping in to run this place if something happened to me or Terry. The business would go down the pan for sure,' she joked.

'Joe's certainly been a great help,' Maria added, acting like she was a family friend, 'we volunteered together at the homeless shelter's festive dinner the other night, but Gloria was unable to make it. I just wanted to pop by and cheer her up a bit. She must be climbing the walls with having to sit around all day, only I've forgotten where Joe said they lived now.'

'Oh she'll certainly appreciate that love and you can take a packet of our homemade ginger cookies with you too.' She went and retrieved a pack from a nearby unit and handed it over to Maria, 'with my compliments love - these are her favourites. You'll find her in one of those fancy houses off Bell Lane. It's the one just past the railway bridge on the right-hand side. Chestnuts or Chestnut something it's called.' By this time, she'd helped Maria carry her order out to the car, making sure it was packed securely in the boot. 'Do give her our best and tell her I'll come over and see her after Christmas as we'll be closed for a few days.' They said their goodbyes leaving Maria to drive off hoping that Gloria Starr would be a lot more receptive than her son.

* * *

Finding Chestnut House had been relatively easy but now she was stood on the threshold, Maria's nerves began to kick in. She gingerly pressed the doorbell and a friendly voice promptly greeted her through the intercom.

'Hello, can I help you?'

'Oh hello …' Maria hesitated, 'I was hoping to see Mrs Starr if possible. I've got something I want to give her.' Having grown up in Christmas Cove, Maria knew that Bell Lane was one of the most desirable places to live in the county, so she was doubly anxious not to mess things up again.

'Ooh that sounds nice; I'm always happy to receive gifts. Come on inside, the door's not locked.' Maria took a deep breath before carefully turning the handle that opened up the impressive solid oak front door. Not easy when attempting to balance a large box containing an uncooked turkey together with a packet of ginger biscuits in the other hand! 'I'm in here love,' Gloria Starr called out and Maria discarded her fur-lined boots in the hallway, before apprehensively joining her in the lounge. As soon as she entered the room, Maria was met by the kindest smile she'd seen in a long time.

'Hello you must be Gloria, I do hope I'm not intruding. My name's Maria and I've come to give you and your son a huge apology.'

'Hello Maria, come and sit down by the fire love; I've been expecting you.'

CHAPTER TEN

It hadn't taken long for Gloria to work out the chaotic misunderstanding that had occurred between Joe and Maria earlier in the week. She'd quickly guessed that Maria had got the two farm shops along Sandy Road confused and therefore knew that sooner or later she would realise her mistake.

When Joe had come home from the homeless shelter's festive dinner a few nights ago, still raging from another altercation with Maria, Gloria had no doubts that if this young woman was prepared to give her time to such a worthy cause, she'd soon realise her mistake and put things right. So it wasn't that surprising to find her turning up on her doorstep out of the blue that day, but it was nevertheless nice.

She listened carefully as Maria's tale of woe unfolded, noticing how animated she became when she talked about Joe – her big, brown eyes widened and her cheeks became quite flushed. When she expressed her frustration that he wouldn't allow her to properly explain herself, Gloria had to stifle her amusement. *They're like two peas in a pod!* Once Maria had unburdened herself and apologised profusely over and over again - despite Gloria assuring her that it wasn't necessary - Gloria encouraged her to take the replacement turkey into the kitchen and put it in the fridge and then suggested she make them a nice cup of tea to accompany the mouth-wateringly tempting ginger biscuits.

'I can't say that I recall your aunt to be honest, where did you say you lived again love?'

'Holly Cottage; it's about five houses along from the church in Poacher's Pocket. The door and window frames are painted a bright blue colour, I'm sure you must have seen it. Most people notice it when they visit the area and we're always getting tourists snapping photographs – people often depict it as a chocolate box house – do you know what I mean?'

'Oh I do know it! Yes, it's all coming back to me now. I did know a couple who lived there, with a small child.' Suddenly her face changed, quickly becoming more serious, 'your Ellen and Tony's girl, aren't you love?' Maria nodded solemnly. She never spoke about her past. 'Oh sweetheart,' she leant forward and patted Maria's hand, 'I knew your mum; we used to go to school together but lost touch once we left, which was just before she had you I guess. It was a sorry state of affairs, I don't suppose you remember her after all this time.' Maria shook her head slowly.

'Not really, I wasn't quite four years old.' Gloria blinked back tears as she recalled how her friend had lost her life after being hit by a drunk driver.

'Terrible business it was too. Despite being in all the papers and constantly reported on the TV, they never manged to find the driver did they?'

'Apparently not. I know my aunt and uncle tried to get it reinvestigated when I was a teenager but nothing came of it.'

'No wonder your aunt's death has rocked your world my love, it must have triggered all sorts of bad memories for you.' She stood up then and went to comfort Maria as she gave way to tears of grief. She'd tried to be strong for so long, but she couldn't hold it back a moment longer. 'Here, why don't I fetch us some more tea?'

It took a few moments to dawn on Maria that Gloria appeared far more mobile than she'd expected her to be. She waited for Gloria to refresh their teacups before mentioning anything. 'It's good to see you up and about, Joe seemed very worried about you. He must be relieved you're on the mend.' Now it was Gloria's turn to appear remorseful.

'Oh Maria, don't think badly of me love,' she retook her seat in the cosy armchair next to the roaring fire, 'I really did take a nasty tumble that day – fell off the step ladder at the farm shop - fell squarely on my hip too and it was agony, sheer agony I tell you. Bev and Linda thought I'd broken it you see, so they called an ambulance and of course, they took me straight to hospital. By the time I'd had all these tests and x-rays, the hospital had already contacted Joe. They made it worse by telling him I wouldn't be able to manage on my own which surprised me I can tell you. I mean, I'm 71 and I've got more energy in me than a festive pack of Duracell batteries!' she jested before concern etched across her face. 'You can imagine how I felt once I got home and realised that I wasn't as mobile as I thought I would be. The pain's been unbearable at times but having Joe home, running around and looking after me has given me the chance to rest up. Only now I'm feeling better and I've got some of my strength back, I don't want to mention anything in case he goes away again; at least not until after the holidays anyhow.' Maria smiled knowingly; it was her turn to offer comfort now.

The newfound friends were enjoying getting to know each other and hadn't realised how long they'd been chatting until Gloria reached to switch the table lamp on as it was beginning to get dark. Maria realised it was time she made her way home before she overstayed her welcome and began gathering their cups and saucers. 'I'd better get going,' she loaded everything onto the tea tray and carried it through to the kitchen, 'I've taken up enough of your time already and I expect Joe will be home soon wanting his dinner.'

'Why don't you stay and join us,' Gloria's eyes glistened, full of hope, 'you said you wanted to apologise to him as well so why not do it sooner rather than later.' Maria couldn't argue with that, especially when she'd put it so charmingly and offered to make them another cup of tea whilst Gloria regaled tales from her and Maria's mum's school days.

They were so ensconced in their conversation that neither of them realised Joe had arrived home until he burst into the lounge. Surprised, Maria looked up to meet his gaze, hopeful to reconcile their differences and begin on a new page but Joe wasn't quite as welcoming as his mother had been. His reaction quickly shattered any hopes she'd harboured. 'Oh good God,' he groaned, 'what the hell are you doing here!'

CHAPTER ELEVEN

'Whatever's got into you Joe?' Gloria ranted. She knew her son was upset following his altercations with Maria – and to be fair, who could blame him – but she hadn't expected him to react quite so rudely towards her. *Someone's clearly rattled.* She attempted to calm the waters by explaining how delighted she was that Maria had come to see her so that she could apologise face-to-face for her mistake as soon as she'd realised what had happened. 'You have to admit Joe, it's an easy mistake for anyone to make. I know we've not had orders muddled like this before, but we've certainly had plenty of people come in and ask for directions to the Old Farm Shop - and vice versa from what Julie's told me over the years.'

'But she practically attacked me, mum, *and* accused me of lying, not to mention dragging poor Katy into the whole affray too. And what about Mrs Winter – she kept giving me evils all night after the performance *she* put on.' Maria was becoming irritated herself now.

'Hang on a minute,' Maria rallied, 'you seem to forget that it was you who attacked *me* remember? And Mrs Winter was right to reprimand you too; you accused me of being a thief!'

'And you stamped on my toes!' he yelled, expressing himself far louder than he'd intended to.

'That's enough Joe!' Gloria cut in, 'there's no need for all this ranting and raving. Why don't we all just calm down and take a breath. I've had a lovely afternoon getting to know Maria and I can assure you that there was never any ill intentions on her part. It's just one of those unfortunate things Joe but it's time to move on from all that now. Listen, why don't I make us all something to eat and then we can spend a lovely evening together.' Maria had already put her coat on by this time though; she didn't want to stay a moment longer where she didn't feel welcome. It took all her strength to stop her chin from wobbling and held back tears as she hugged Gloria goodbye and thanked her for a lovely afternoon. After promising to visit again soon, she quietly let herself out of the front door before bursting into tears.

The snow had begun falling again and she had to take a moment to clear the windows before she could get into her car and drive away. On the coastal road back home, Maria's headlights illuminated the beach enough for her to see waves crashing onto the cliff face which only made it harder to forget the unpleasant scene she'd just walked away from.

CHAPTER TWELVE

You could cut through the atmosphere between Gloria and Joe with a knife once Maria had left. Apart from the table lamp Gloria had switched on earlier that afternoon, the only other light flooding in through the lounge windows was from the headlights of Maria's car, which soon diminished as she slowly made her way down the drive and disappeared out onto Bell Lane.

Gloria stared into the glowing embers of the fire, speechless. There was so much that she wanted to say but knew that silence was golden in that moment. The chunky, silver tinsel she'd draped across the mantel piece reflected the glow from the fire prompting her to remember that she'd not yet switched the Christmas tree lights on. The twinkling from the tiny, multi-coloured lights always raised her spirits but on second thoughts, it was probably best to leave it for now. She wasn't certain anything could lift the gloom following Maria's impromptu exit.

Her stomach rumbled noisily reminding her that they'd not eaten but it was too late to cook a meal at that time of night. 'Why don't you go and jump in the shower Joe,' she suggested, knowing it would give him an opportunity to gather his thoughts, 'and I'll make us a sandwich and a cup of tea.' He nodded absentmindedly and slowly made his way upstairs whilst Gloria shuffled towards the kitchen.

Her mind was elsewhere as she filled the kettle and put it on to boil before turning her attention to spreading mustard onto slices of fresh, white bread. Then she added sliced tomatoes, a sprinkling of seasoning and thick slices of best ham. She cut the sandwiches into neat triangles and poured hot water over the tea bags she'd already popped into the pot. It took her a couple of trips to carry everything into the lounge and she took time to set the dishes out neatly onto the coffee table. Her hip had become quite sore by this time, and she knew she'd overdone things. She poured out two cups of tea, adding sugar to Joe's cup. Gloria settled back into her cosy armchair just as Joe burst back through the lounge door, shrugging on his winter coat.

'I'm going to drive over and see her,' he announced dramatically, 'I feel terrible about my behaviour – my actions couldn't be further from my intentions,' he shook his head, clearly disappointed by his earlier outburst, 'I want a chance to speak to her and explain properly; where did you say she lived?' Gloria looked up aghast; her heart swelled with pride. Although she wished nothing more than for these two to get their act together, Gloria was astute enough to know that it had been a long day for them all. Despite Joe's best intentions, it was better to let things settle for a bit.

'You can't go out like that Joe,' she chided, 'your hair's still wet and besides, it's almost 10 pm. I don't think it's going to benefit anyone trying to resolve this tonight. Why don't you leave it until tomorrow, eh love?' Joe began to pace the floor.

'I don't want to leave it like this though,' he exclaimed, 'I didn't mean to react like that. It was just - finding her here at our home – I hadn't expected it and didn't know what to think and well, I'm angry with myself now at the way I spoke to her. I'd wished things would have gone differently that's all.'

'She's a nice girl Joe. It takes a lot of courage to admit when you're in the wrong and Maria just wanted to put things right again. I'm sure you two can quickly iron out this misunderstanding but tonight's not the best time to tackle it, trust me. Leave it until the morning when you can look at it again through fresh eyes.' Reluctantly, Joe knew his mother was right and shrugged off his coat which he hung back up in the cloakroom before returning to drink his tea. He couldn't face anything to eat as his stomach was in knots. It wasn't just about wanting to apologise for his bad behaviour though. There was something about Maria that had got under his skin from the moment their eyes had met across the farm shop counter.

Inwardly, he'd been thrilled to find her cosied up on their sofa, with her legs tucked beneath her. She clearly felt right at home. As the recollection of how her bright smile had soon dissolved into a look of hurt following his outburst, he felt an icy grip clutch at his heart and it pained him. He was mortified. *How could I have got it so wrong?*

'I won't lie mum, it's been a hell of a day all round which wasn't helped much by Bev and Linda; what a duo those two are! They've certainly kept me on my toes – I don't know how you cope with running that busy shop *and* managing the staff – it's exhausting.' Gloria smiled knowingly.

'To tell you the truth Joe, we could do with hiring a couple of additional shop assistants. Since they built that big housing estate on the south side of Christmas Cove, business has really picked up and that's without the increase in folk who come seeking out our organic range. When I introduced the delicatessen, that really kicked things off – far more than I'd anticipated. There's a lot of improvements that need to be made first though and it's something I'd planned to look at in the New Year. In the meantime, it's worth remembering that it's people like Bev and Linda that have kept me going all these years. I know they can be difficult – and a bit awkward – but they'd give you the shirt off their backs if it'd help you, they really would. It might surprise you to know they're not without their own problems too.' Joe was intrigued to hear this and absentmindedly reached for a ham sandwich, keen for Gloria to reveal more.

'Bev's eldest boy has been in all sorts of trouble over the years. His dad got him a job on a building site on an apprenticeship, you know what I mean, and he walked out after a couple of weeks and started hanging out with this right load of timewasters. I've had her sitting where you are now in floods of tears over his shenanigans I can tell you. He was in court just last week for possession of something or another and he was lucky to get away with a suspended sentence. Bev almost had kittens over it. Well, as you can imagine it's been enough to put a rocket up his you-know-what and he's back on the building site now thank God. Let's just hope he sticks at it.' Joe was astounded. With the way Bev was strutting about earlier, you'd never had guessed she was carrying such a huge burden. 'And as for Linda, well her husband leads that poor woman a merry dance, but you can't tell her. He's always down the pub up to goodness knows what whilst she's at home looking after the kids. Now her own children have grown up and had kids of their own, they dump them on her whilst they're off enjoying life and poor old Linda is stuck at home. I'd give her a full-time job at the drop of a hat if I knew she'd take it but Ronnie – her husband – will only let her do a few hours here and there. I don't know how she sticks it. Your father would never have treated me like that. Makes me thankful every day for what we had, even though he's no longer with us. I miss him like crazy of course but we did have a good life together.' Listening to his mum had given Joe much food for thought and he realised he'd been too quick in making judgements about his co-workers without having a clue to the personal issues they might be battling with. This again reminded him of Maria and made him even more determined to straighten things out with her. *Who knows, we might even become good friends?* But deep down, Joe knew he'd like more than just a friendship. Gloria began clearing the table and Joe stood up to take over.

'You get off to bed mum, I'll take care of this, it's the least I can do.' She patted him gratefully on the arm.

'Don't beat yourself up about it too much Joe, you're a good son and I'm really proud of you. I know you'll sort this out.' Then an idea popped into her head, 'it'd be nice to invite Maria to join us for Christmas especially as she's spending it on her own this year. You might think about that when you go and see her tomorrow, but I'll leave it for you to decide. Goodnight.' Joe felt like he was bouncing on air as he shuttled the dishes to the kitchen and switched everything off before heading upstairs to bed, his heart full of hope. *Perhaps this Christmas will be one to remember for all the right reasons after all.*

CHAPTER THIRTEEN

Maria sipped her coffee, relishing the warmth from the mug as she cradled it in her hands. She was sitting at her favourite spot – her work desk – which she'd deliberately placed in front of the picturesque window that presented a perfect view of the village green from beyond Holly Cottage's front garden.

There were several children playing outside in the snow and she'd watched them finish building a snowman before scooping up gloved hands full of snow and shaping it into small balls to throw playfully at each other. She was sorely tempted to humour her inner child and join them but decided to settle for a bird's eye view instead. Fresh snow had begun falling again during the past hour, reminding her of the treacherous journey she'd endured driving back from Chestnut House the evening before.

She sighed deeply. She'd not had the best night's sleep and running the events of last night through her mind again and again wasn't helping. She rolled her eyes in frustration over the way she'd reacted to Joe, who was clearly not best pleased at having arrived home only to discover her cosied up on the sofa, drinking tea and chatting with his mother.

She wished she'd allowed him more time to vent his frustrations at her so that she could have had the opportunity to properly explain herself. She kept replaying the events of the past week over and over, now realising that she should have at least telephoned him at the shop first instead of choosing to go straight to see his mother. Certainly if she had the chance again, she deal with the situation completely differently. *Hindsight is a wonderful thing Maria!*

Even though they'd locked horns at the farm shop and had that tussle with the cooked turkey at the homeless shelter, Maria thought she'd seen a playful twinkle in his eye and a smirk playing on his lips. If she was completely honest, she'd acted up a bit and been playfully high-spirited herself, somewhat enjoying their fractious interactions. She blushed then, knowing full well that him being easy on the eye had played a big part in it all too.

In the past, when she used to accompany Aunt Ellen to collect the festive order from the Old Farm Shop, they'd only ever met and interacted with Julie. She was always incredibly welcoming, and they looked forward to a hot drink and mince pie whilst they enjoyed a catch-up. So it was understandable, Maria reasoned with herself, that when she arrived at Starr's Farm Shop – albeit the wrong one – she was somewhat distracted by the tall, dark handsome stranger with the sparkly blue eyes that she was not expecting to greet her from behind the counter. *Oh well, it's too late now,* she sighed again and went through to the kitchen to make a fresh brew.

The radio was still playing to itself and promptly claimed her attention.

Residents of Christmas Cove and the surrounding areas are being advised to avoid all unnecessary travel following the Met Office warnings for snow and high winds leading to possible blizzard conditions …

Maria was thankful that she'd already completed her shopping and hoped she'd still be able to make it across the green to join Midnight Mass at the local church. *Another tradition I enjoyed with Aunt Ellen.* She silently prayed that this ritual wouldn't end in chaos.

Her thoughts returned to Gloria. She'd so enjoyed getting to know her yesterday and was sorely tempted to pick up the telephone and call her. But as the situation was still raw, she decided to leave it for the time being and returned her focus to an idea she'd had for a new range of buttons instead.

CHAPTER FOURTEEN

A flutter of excitement rippled through Joe as he awoke that morning; *it's Christmas Eve!* He always enjoyed the holidays and threw himself into the season of goodwill with gusto. Having woken up bright and early, he decided to skip breakfast knowing the farm shop café was planning to serve up cooked breakfasts that morning. He was looking forward to tucking into a hot sausage and bacon sandwich, *a nice change from my usual bowl of muesli*. He settled for a cup of tea instead, making one for Gloria which he placed on a tray together with two slices of hot, generously buttered toast.

'Morning mum,' he chirped merrily as he set the tray down on the bed next to her and walked across the room to open up the bedroom curtains. The bright, morning light flooded in, causing him to squint before he turned his attention back to Gloria. 'How are you feeling today? I thought I heard you get up in the night?' Gloria shuffled herself into an upright position, whilst Joe leaned down and helped puff the pillows up around her until she felt more comfortable.

'It wasn't the best night love.' A painful expression was etched onto her face, filling Joe with concern. He hated that his behaviour the evening before had no doubt added to her angst too. 'I had to get a couple of my pills, the pain in my hip was terrible. I feel a bit better now, but I think I'll stay here for a while. Switch the telly on for me would you love?' Joe grabbed the remote and as the set burst into life their attention was drawn to the chaos unfolding in other parts of the country due to the bad weather. 'Oh dear

Joe,' Gloria nodded towards the ticker at the bottom of the news channel screen, 'look at that — it says we've got that bad weather coming here later. You might have to close up early.' She looked up at him, her face full of concern, 'best you get off love if you don't mind me saying so. You have got rather a lot of orders to get ready today.' Joe was quick to agree.

'Don't forget that I'm planning to stop by Maria's on the way home as well, but I'll call you and let you know.'

'Mind you do but if the weather gets that bad Joe, you'll have to leave it for today and perhaps ring her later instead, okay?' Joe nodded and kissed her fondly on the cheek, but he wasn't really listening. His mind had been well and truly made up on that score already. He'd rehearsed what he planned to say enough times now and if he didn't get it all out sometime soon, he feared he might burst!

'Call me if you need anything mum and *please*, don't worry about the housework either. I just want you to rest so that your pain eases up. You'll need all your energy to cook that huge turkey Maria brought round last night anyway.' She smiled warmly at his gentle teasing and gave a little wave as he left, before returning her focus back to the morning news.

* * *

When Joe pulled up at the farm shop a half hour or so later, he cut the engine and took a moment to soak up the view. Being situated on the edge of farmland, the shop was surrounded by fields which were now all covered in a thick blanket of white snow. It reminded Joe of a scene from one of the many Christmas cards they'd received both at the shop and at home, and he couldn't resist taking out his mobile phone to capture a few pictures before heading inside to begin what he knew was going to be a chaotic day.

The aroma of salty bacon filled the air. His stomach rumbled as he made his way to the office to hang up his coat and scarf and put on his shopkeeper's tabard, branded with the Starr's Farm Shop logo. It was still early and he could hear Bev, Linda and Katy chattering away excitedly in the café. 'Morning ladies,' he greeted cheerfully as he went to join them.

'Morning Joe!' they chorused together and Bev got up to fetch his sandwich and a cup of steaming hot coffee, which she placed on the table in front of him as he sat down.

'Oh thanks Bev, I've been really looking forward to this.' He added in a few dollops of tomato ketchup before tucking in.

'Good news Joe,' Katy smiled brightly, 'we found our Benji last night. My dad's right made up he is and even drove me to work today so I didn't have to catch the bus.'

'That is great news,' Joe managed to gasp between mouthfuls, savouring the rare treat, 'where did you find him then?'

'You won't believe this - he got stuck in our neighbours' garage. They've been away delivering Christmas presents to family they've got up north and they reckon he must have slipped inside and hid when they were loading up the car.'

'I'm surprised someone didn't hear him barking,' Linda tutted, 'poor thing, he must have barked himself hoarse.'

'Yeah, he definitely didn't sound like his usual self, that's for sure but don't forget Linda, there's a good distance between our house and the nearest neighbour. We're right out in the sticks there so we didn't hear a thing. Not to worry though as my dad's taking him to the vet this morning to get him checked over so hopefully he'll soon be back to his mischievous self again.'

'Talking of mischievousness, let's hope we don't get any more drama today, eh Joe? Katy was telling us all about that woman who came in last week, what a right commotion that was.' Joe stopped eating and wiped the remnants of ketchup from the corners of his mouth with a paper napkin. His audience sensed they'd hit a raw spot, but Joe was determined not to let it spoil his good mood. He nonchalantly brushed off the incident as being nothing more than a simple misunderstanding.

'But you said she'd turned up at that homeless shelter thing you went to and stole your turkey!' Katy exclaimed, desperate to make the incident far more dramatic than it was. Joe rolled his eyes knowing full well she wasn't far from the truth.

'Well, I'm embarrassed to admit that's my bad – I clearly embellished the situation far more than I intended to, sorry about that Katy. It was honestly nothing more than a storm in a teacup - just a simple misunderstanding - I'm sure we've all experienced plenty of those.' He was certain not to make eye contact with any of them fearing he might give away the insight into their own trials and tribulations his mother had shared with him the previous evening. He really didn't want to get involved in *that*.

He wasn't immediately aware of the reaction from Bev and Linda to his explanation who were now playfully nudging each other, assuming he might have been trying to impress Katy with his bragging because he was sweet on her. Katy noticed it too and a bright red blush crept into her cheeks causing her to giggle shyly. Joe looked from one to the other of them, confused by their reaction and then suddenly caught on causing his own cheeks to flush a nice shade of crimson. 'Hang about, let's not get the wrong idea here,' he held up his hand in protest, 'no offence Katy but my heart belongs to someone else. I'm sure a nice girl like you has plenty of suitors to choose from anyway.'

'Huh, you should be so lucky,' she responded tartly, her ego a tad bruised, 'I have got a boyfriend as it happens and now that our Benji's turned up my dad says I can bring him home for tea on Boxing Day.' Bev and Linda could hardly draw breath demanding to know all the ins and outs of this new relationship which thankfully drew their attention away from Joe and left him to enjoy his food in peace.

He finished up his sandwich and drank the last of his coffee, 'that was a fabulous breakfast Bev, thank you. If that's a taste of what's on offer on the menu today, then our customers are in for a real treat.' Bev basked in her moment of glory. 'I guess the rest of us better get our own act together now and make a start on the orders.' The sound of chair legs scraping across the wooden floor resounded around the room as they all stood up and set about their tasks.

Just before opening, Joe took a moment to ensure that everything was in order. The fairy lights were all switched on, Christmas carols were ringing out from the sound system and all the orders were ready and waiting to be collected. He gathered the small group together and handed each of them a festive novelty hat which made them laugh and playfully tease each other. Everyone was in high spirits as Joe opened up the doors – he only hoped it would stay that way.

CHAPTER FIFTEEN

It was the coldest day of winter so far and the great snowfall that was predicted had begun. The howling wind was causing the windows to rattle in their frames and Maria stoked up the fire again having decided to pack away her work for the day and make herself something to eat. She had a jacket potato warming in the oven that she'd planned to enjoy with homemade turkey chilli.

As she tidied her desk, she noticed that the village green had fallen silent. She wasn't entirely sure when the children had left but it must have been a while ago as a fresh blanket of snow had almost covered the ruts and footprints created when they were running around and playing out there earlier.

As Maria began serving up her lunch, the lights flickered. She stopped what she was doing and went in search of some candles in case the power went out. There was an old oak dresser that occupied almost the whole of the back wall in the cosy lounge, where she quickly located a selection of candles, a box of matches and even a battery operated torch. She returned to the kitchen with them, switching the radio on along the way. Sitting down to enjoy her food, she soon became so absorbed with her thoughts that it was little wonder she shrieked in surprise when the telephone sprang into life, the ringer resounding noisily around the room. Her cutlery clanged against the side of the bowl before she reached to answer it.

'Is that you Maria love? It's Gloria, I do hope you don't mind me calling you only I just had to check how you were feeling after last night.' A huge smile swept across Maria's face at the sound of Gloria's voice.

'It's lovely to hear from you, I've been thinking about you – and Joe too of course. I feel a bit silly now about turning up out of the blue like that. I am sorry. If I'd come home and found a stranger cosied up on the sofa talking to Aunt Ellen, I'm sure I would have reacted in just the same way – if not worse truth be told!' she laughed and Gloria relaxed a little hearing that she'd obviously taken the time to think through the situation again.

'That's true I suppose, although you're not exactly a stranger – not to Joe anyhow – but I take your point. Personally, I applaud you Maria for seeking me out. That takes guts and like you, I would have wanted to resolve things as quickly as possible too, so don't feel bad about that. The thing is love, Joe's also had time to think and whilst I don't want to spoil anything, I know he's planning on coming over to see you after work tonight to apologise. He feels terrible about the way he acted, as well he should and I told him that as well.' Maria's heart skipped a beat. A wave of excitement surged through her but then her stomach knotted with anxiety. 'I said to him, you both need your heads banging together you do because I think we all know what's really going on here and I want nothing more than to see you both happy – whatever path that takes - only I've been watching the news all morning and it's not looking good for Christmas Cove at all. The weather's going to hit us hard by the time Joe closes up tonight and if I know my Joe, I doubt he'll let that stop him trying to drive over to you.' Maria wasn't certain what exactly it was that Gloria was asking of her, so she continued to listen attentively. 'I was wondering if you'd considering phoning him at the shop instead – it's almost time for his lunch break - and you could talk things over with him, make out like you'd just called on the off chance that he'd be free. What do you think?' Maria didn't need to be asked twice.

'Actually I think that's a great idea. I've been mentally berating myself for walking away like that last night,' she paused before adding, 'and I really appreciate you taking the time to call and share Joe's intentions. I want nothing more than a chance to talk this through with him properly. Give me a minute to gather my thoughts and I'll give you a call back later and let you know how I get on.' After exchanging heartfelt goodbyes, Maria replaced the handset and clicked the radio off so she could take stock for a moment or two. She certainly wasn't averse to speaking to Joe on the telephone, it was something that had crossed her mind several times that day already. But she was mindful that they'd already suffered several chaotic misunderstandings, *perhaps a face-to-face meeting would work out far better.*

She checked the time, *1 pm.* She knew the store was due to stay open until 6 pm, although she wondered if they would have to consider closing earlier given the dire weather forecast. However, all things considered she deduced that would still give her plenty of time to drive over to see Joe and make it safely back home before the storm blew in. Well, that's what she anticipated anyhow.

CHAPTER SIXTEEN

The energy in the farm shop was bouncing off the walls as Joe and his small team continued to exchange excited banter whilst attending to their customers. It appeared that most people had ventured out that morning in an attempt to avoid the storm and at one stage, the queue was almost out of the door. Word soon got around that delicious, home cooked breakfasts were being served in the seasonal café and Joe's idea began to pay dividends as hungry customers took advantage of a hot drink and something to eat whilst they waited and gave the farm shop coffers an unexpected boost! Even Linda had surpassed herself by taking time out of the café every now and then to ensure the shelves were kept stocked and replenish the wire baskets for new customers to reuse again. By lunchtime, all the orders had been collected and Joe couldn't be happier. His assistants made him proud.

Despite knowing in advance that Gloria had arranged for a festive hamper with non-perishable goods to be delivered to each of their homes – something that she organised every year – during his lunch break he took time out to prepare an additional cash bonus for each of them to show his appreciation for all the extra effort and hard work they'd put in, especially whilst Gloria was recuperating at home.

'Look at that!' Bev gasped, suddenly claiming his attention and causing him to leave the office to investigate further. 'It's turned proper nasty out there now, just listen to that wind!' Linda and Katy joined her by the large window at the front of the store where they huddled together, transfixed as huge snowflakes began falling at an increased rate. The wind was howling fiercely and bits of debris were being blown about by the strong wind. Joe stood behind them unable to believe his eyes.

'Good heavens! When did all that kick off,' he was astonished at the rate the snow was coming down, 'I didn't think it would be as severe as this.' They turned and looked cautiously at each other. Joe's concerns were growing too. He was well aware that the forecast had predicted worse to come and with this in mind, he quickly came to a decision, 'I think it's best if you all head off home now before it gets any worse,' he announced, 'none of us wants to get stuck here, especially on Christmas Eve.'

'But we can't leave you to cope on your own Joe, how are you going to manage? Last Christmas Eve it went mad just after 5 pm, when everyone left work and decided to do a last bit of shopping on the way home.'

'It wasn't snowing like this though Linda so I don't think many people are going to want to venture out now. At least all the orders have been collected, so I'll just stay for the next hour or so in case of any stragglers then head home myself. My 4x4 out there should get me safely through anything so I'll be okay. You all just concentrate on getting yourselves home safely and if you do happen to get stuck, give me a call.' The trio didn't need telling twice and made a mad dash over to the staff room in order to collect their belongings.

'I don't suppose there's room for me in your car is there Linda?' Katy looked over at her colleague with anxious eyes, 'only my dad was supposed to be picking me up later and I don't fancy trying to walk to the bus stop in this.'

'Of course love, get your coat on and wrap up warm – it can take a while for my old banger to heat up can't it Bev?'

Joe promptly remembered the gift envelopes he'd prepared for each of them just in time, which momentarily lifted their spirits and prompted them to exchange hugs and merry Christmas wishes. Only once outside did it really occur to them just how treacherous the roads were, and Linda exchanged further worried glances with Bev before they all got into her car. Joe watched them drive carefully away having since decided that he might as well clear up and head home sooner rather than later himself.

CHAPTER SEVENTEEN

Although it had begun to snow heavily, driving out of Poacher's Pocket wasn't too challenging until Maria was about half-way along the coastal road. The strong winds blasted the sides of her small car, causing it to sway like the choppy waves that were breaking on the rocks and threatening the sea wall. With her wipers battling the torrent of snow clouding the windscreen, Maria clasped hold of the steering wheel and focussed hard on what she could see of the road ahead.

She took solace that she wasn't the only person to venture out that afternoon as she passed by several other vehicles. Only she hadn't considered that most of these people were making their way safely home.

When she reached the car park of Starr's Farm Shop, she was surprised to discover only one other vehicle parked there. It was covered in snow and looked like it had been abandoned, *oh no, don't tell me he's closed up already!* But the lights were on in the shop convincing her that there was someone at home. She brought her car to a slow halt and prepared to do battle with the elements.

The wind was vociferous and she had to hang on tight to the car door, fearing that it would be blown off before closing it securely and heading towards the front doors. Blasts of icy snow stung like tiny needles and she pulled her woolly scarf up further to protect her eyes and face as she trudged forward with her head dipped. The powdery snow had already begun to drift and was gathering against the front steps, getting deeper and deeper and almost completely disguising their existence. Maria plodded forward, totally clueless of the impending danger and promptly misjudged her footing. As she brought her boot down, she found herself suddenly propelled forward. A searing pain shot through her ankle and up her leg before she face-planted the ground.

It took a split second before the realisation of what had just occurred set in. Maria groaned noisily and attempted to push herself upright again, but the pain in her leg and ankle was making the motion difficult. 'Aaaaarrgghhhh!' she screamed out loud in pain and frustration, 'is there anybody there – I need help!'

CHAPTER EIGHTEEN

Having shut down the seasonal café and tidied up the shop, Joe went to collect the bags of festive goodies he had set aside for their own Christmas celebrations. He'd included an extra box of luxury mince pies and some handmade chocolates which he hoped Maria would enjoy, *but I need to invite her to join us first.*

Although the turn in the weather had genuinely concerned Joe, he couldn't help but feel it presented an opportunity to sort out his dis-ease with Maria sooner rather than later. So, he grabbed his winter coat from the cloakroom and was shaking it on over his thick wool jumper when something caught his attention. It wasn't that easy to hear above the noise of the howling wind and snow lashing against the roof and the sides of the building, but he was certain he heard something.

He cautiously peered out of the office door and then stepped back into the shop, looking around before his eyes settled on the front doors. He quickly grabbed the keys, realising that he'd switched off the automatic doors earlier and went to assist the very distressed figure rolling around on the floor outside.

As the doors swished opened, he rushed forward and was gobsmacked at coming face-to-face with Maria. 'Oh good God,' he groaned, 'what the hell are you doing here!'

CHAPTER NINETEEN

Maria was fuming! It appeared by Joe's reaction that he'd learnt nothing from their altercation the previous night and she glared angrily at him. 'Seriously? You want to go there again, do you?' Having realised he'd engaged his mouth before his brain again, Joe looked back at her coyly before a smile sheepishly danced across his face.

'I clearly need a better repertoire,' he jested, 'it's just ...' he raised his hands in an upward gesture, somewhat flummoxed, 'of all the people to find crumpled up in a heap on the doorstep, I can honestly say I did not expect it to be you!' Maria had to laugh along with him.

'Well, can you at least help me up. I think I might have twisted my ankle because it's hurting like crazy and I'm struggling to stand.' A concerned look soon wiped the smile off Joe's face as he bent forward and placed his arms around her. It didn't take much to lift her back onto her feet, but he'd not anticipated coming quite so up close and personal. Their eyes locked and a deep feeling of attraction surged through him.

'Err ...,' he mumbled, attempting to refocus his attention to the task in hand, 'let's get you safely inside shall we and then we can take a look at what's happened.' Keeping a firm arm around her waist, he guided Maria through the front doors and into the back office where he settled her onto the nearest chair. She slipped off her hat and unwound her scarf grateful to be out of the blustery snow showers. 'It might be an idea to take that wet coat off,' Joe suggested, and went to assist her out of it. He hung it up and turned on the electric fan heater to help dry it out. 'Now, let's take a look at that foot, is it okay if I unzip your boot?' Maria nodded gratefully and appreciated his assistance as he carefully pulled the zipper on the side of the boot and slipped it off before slowly removing the thick, woollen navy sock beneath.

'Oh!' They said in unison as they took in the sight of her red and swollen ankle. Maria bit the edge of her lip and Joe was quick to reassure her.

'I expect you've just sprained it is all,' he got up and went over to the first aid cabinet that was situated on the office wall. 'We've got a stock of support bandages in here – health and safety and all that.' She watched him select and unpack a suitable dressing before tenderly cradling her ankle ready to wrap it in the elasticated cotton dressing. 'There you go,' he smiled, standing up once her ankle was secured, 'that should help until we get you seen by minor injuries,' causing them to exchange looks again but this time anxious ones!

'Oh? Do you think it's as bad as that? Only I'm not sure I can drive, especially in this state?.'

'I wouldn't let you anyway,' Joe assured her, 'I meant for me to drive you. Just give me a few moments to finish locking up and then we'll leave.' The phone began to ring harshly and Joe snatched it up, maintaining his focus on his patient. 'Oh it's you mum, is everything alright?' Maria's eyes widened in horror at the realisation of who the caller was. Gloria had specifically asked her to telephone Joe herself and Maria knew his mother wasn't going to be impressed by her decision to do elsewise.

'Sorry Joe, I don't think I heard you right,' Gloria gasped in disbelief, 'only I thought you said that Maria was with you and had fallen and hurt her ankle?'

'That's what I said mum and looking at the size of the swelling, I think she should go to the emergency room at Christmas Cove minor injuries unit.'

'Huh!' she retorted, 'good luck with that love, have you looked out the window? It's chaos out there. I've just got off the phone from speaking to Linda and she said they had a nightmare journey home so I put the news on. The coastal road is completely blocked now, there's cars abandoned everywhere. I don't know how you're going to get back home Joe, let alone minor injuries.' Gloria began to fret then, 'it's not broken is it Joe? How's she feeling?' Joe glanced back across the room at Maria, who gave a timid wave wondering if Gloria had spilled the beans yet. 'Well she looks bright enough, I'll keep an eye on her but what are we supposed to do now if we can't get out of here.'

'I suggest you call the non-emergency line and ask them for advice. You'll not be the only ones but at least you're in the warm – think of those out there, stuck in their cars or worse. Anyway, let me know how you get on, and Joe,' she paused for effect, 'has it occurred to you why Maria ventured out there in the first place?' She ended the call before he had a chance to respond.

'Riiiiggghhhttt …' Joe rubbed the palms of his hands together nervously, 'the good news is that mum and the shop staff are all safely tucked away at home …' Maria was eyeing him carefully wondering if Gloria had divulged the details of their earlier telephone conversation. 'And the *bad* news is that we might have to stay here just a bit longer.'

'What?' Maria sat up straight, but the action promptly made her wince, 'what's going on?'

'It appears that the weather has caused havoc and the coastal road is blocked. My guess is that even if we manage to get out of here and reach that far, we won't stand a chance getting through. I'm going to call through to the emergency services and try and find out more information.'

Frustrated, Maria could only sit and listen as Joe dialled the three-digit non-emergency number and waited for his call to be answered. She shivered as the air began to grow chilly, despite the heat from the fan heater Joe had switched on earlier. He caught sight of her and juggled with slipping off his own coat which he passed to her just as an operator came onto the line. She accepted it gratefully and wrapped it around her, soaking up the lingering aroma from Joe's cologne. She clung onto it dreamily before he cut into the thoughts.

'Well that went well – not!' He folded his arms across his chest and leaned up against the desk, 'it looks like we might be here a while I'm afraid. Mum was right when she said it was chaotic out there – there's been a major crash on the other side of Christmas Cove and the emergency services are working together to try and sort that out *and* rescue people who have become stranded. She said that it could take ages before they clear the roads. I guess we'd better make ourselves comfortable.' Maria nodded and couldn't help thinking that she'd set off with such good intentions in wanting to resolve their angst. She had certainly not anticipated that they'd end up getting snowed-in together, *and on Christmas Eve too!*

Joe busied himself with re-locking the automatic doors and then headed into the café to collect one of the comfy armchairs which he carried back into the office. 'Here you are,' he set it down next to the heater which he then turned around to blow air back into the room, 'you should find this a bit more comfortable, and you can then put your feet up on this.' He helped her to change seats and place her feet on the one she'd vacated. He then went to fetch a comfy chair for himself. 'May as well make ourselves at home for a bit.' She watched him fill the kettle and switch it on thinking how surreal it all seemed. A little over a week ago she didn't even know Joe existed and now she was here, cosied up in the back office of the local farm shop with him. 'What's tickled you,' Joe caught sight of the smile on her face as he poured hot water into two cups containing freeze dried coffee granules.

'I was just thinking how weird this is, us together seeking refuge from the elements. Believe it or not a few weeks ago I was living in the big city and looking forward to spending the festive season with Aunt Ellen.' A wave of emotion surged deep in the pit of her stomach and tears sprang to her eyes. 'Oh I wasn't expecting that, sorry.' Joe came over and knelt down beside her.

'You don't need to apologise,' he soothed, 'I know you're grieving which is why I'm even more cross with myself at overreacting the way I did last night. In fact,' he looked up to meet her gaze, 'I was planning on coming over to see you this afternoon. I sent the others home early once the weather had turned nasty and thought I'd be able to see you and have us home again before all that kicked-off.' Maria wondered if she'd heard him right then, ... *us home?* and opened her mouth to clarify when Joe was reminded of the last thing Gloria had said during her phone call, adding 'which reminds me, what caused you to venture out this way?' Maria closed her mouth and then opened it again, then grimaced awkwardly.

'I came to see you actually. I wanted to apologise about going off in a huff last night and hoped we could talk things through.' He gathered up her hands into his.

'Oh Maria, what are we like?' They laughed together, 'it's me that should be apologising anyway. I don't know,' he shook his head as if the action would straighten up the thoughts he was still struggling to think through, 'if I'm honest, you caught my attention the moment you appeared. I just hadn't expected for things to kick off like that. When I went to collect mum's order and found it had gone missing, I was completely baffled. I thought for one moment I was going crazy!' he laughed again, 'then when I walked into the homeless shelter's kitchen – I was already a bag of nerves having to stand in for mum – but seeing that box I just flipped and finding out it was you who'd taken it, well part of me was annoyed and the other part,' he searched for her gaze again, 'couldn't believe that our paths had crossed again. I was secretly delighted. All I can offer in defence of my foolish behaviour is that I became a little tongue-tied.'

'And I was totally *Starr* struck.' Whilst spoken in jest, something about the way Maria said it caused them to lock eyes. A thrill shot through Joe causing his heart to beat faster as he leaned forward and tentatively touched her lips softly with his. Maria moved further towards him, allowing his arms to tighten around her, drawing her closer as he pressed his mouth firmly against hers. They were momentarily lost in a long, deep kiss until Joe reluctantly pulled away, 'I've been wanting to do that for a while,' he murmured gently before Maria pulled him back towards her again.

EPILOGUE

'Cheers!' Gloria jollied as she raised her glass, 'here's to a merry Christmas!' Joe and Maria giggled before joining in the toast. They'd not been able to wipe the smile off Gloria's face since arriving back to Chestnut House late last night. She feasted her eyes around the table. 'This is a lovely spread Joe,' she complimented him, helping herself to crispy roast potatoes before passing the bowl towards Maria, 'and it's lovely to have you to share it with this year too. How's that ankle of yours holding up?'

When the emergency services had finally cleared the road last night, Joe had driven Maria to the Christmas Cove minor injury unit where an x-ray confirmed the fracture. She was now sporting a bright pink fibre plaster cast.

'It feels much better today thank you. I'm just glad that Joe was around to help me. When I first arrived at the shop yesterday, I thought it was deserted.'

'Oh don't worry about that love,' Gloria nodded towards her son, 'if he hadn't have been there, he'd have been on his way to see you anyhow. I'm just glad you two have finally seen what I saw from the beginning. He's not the brightest star when it comes to romance.' Realising her unintentional quip relating to Maria and Joe's surnames, Bright and Starr, they all fell about laughing.

'Honestly mum, you are funny,' Joe looked across the table at her fondly and then returned his gaze to Maria, 'but I have to say that this Christmas has brought us the brightest star ever!'

Other books by
Tina-Marie Miller

The Hamptons Series:

Everything Happens For A Reason, Book 1

The Curious Miss Fortune, Book 2

Fame and Fortune, Book 3

The Chateau of Second Chances

Printed by Amazon Italia Logistica S.r.l.
Torrazza Piemonte (TO), Italy

42570962R00052